AMANDA PIG
AND THE
AWFUL, SCARY
MONSTER

Jean Van Leeuwen

PICTURES BY

ANN SCHWENINGER

To Elizabeth,
who had monsters
J.V.L.

For Meg
A.S.

PUFFIN BOOKS
Published by Penguin Group
Penguin Young Readers Group,
345 Hudson Street, New York, New York 10014, U.S.A.
Penguin Books Ltd, 80 Strand, London WC2R ORL, England
Penguin Books Australia Ltd, 250 Camberwell Road, Camberwell, Victoria 3124, Australia
Penguin Books Canada Ltd, 10 Alcorn Avenue, Toronto, Ontario, Canada M4V 3B2
Penguin Books (N.Z.) Ltd, 182-190 Wairau Road, Auckland 10, New Zealand

First published in the United States of America by Phyllis Fogelman Books,
an imprint of Penguin Putnam Books for Young Readers, 2003
Published by Puffin Books, a division of Penguin Young Readers Group, 2004

3 5 7 9 10 8 6 4 2

THE LIBRARY OF CONGRESS HAS CATALOGED THE PHYLLIS FOGELMAN EDITION AS FOLLOWS:
Van Leeuwen, Jean.
Amanda Pig and the awful, scary monster / Jean Van Leeuwen; pictures by Ann Schweninger.
p. cm.
Summary: Amanda sees monsters at night, but her parents and brother
find different ways to convince her that there are no monsters.
ISBN: 0-8037-2766-6 (hc)
[1. Monsters—Fiction. 2. Bedtime—Fiction. 3. Fear—Fiction. 4. Pigs—Fiction.]
I. Schweninger, Ann, ill. II. Title. PZ7.V275 Am 2003 [E]—dc21 2001033519

Puffin Easy-to-Read ISBN 0-14-240203-6
Puffin® and Easy-to-Read® are registered trademarks of Penguin Group (USA) Inc.

Manufactured in China
The full-color artwork was prepared using carbon pencil, colored pencils, and watercolor washes.

Reading Level 2.0

CONTENTS

THE MONSTER

"Look at the moon," said Father.

Amanda looked up into the sky.

There was the roundest, fattest,

brightest moon she had ever seen.

"Moon," she said.

What a round, fat, wonderful word.

A poem popped into her head.

"The moon," she said,

"is like a yellow balloon."

"Hey," said Oliver. "That's good."

That was when Amanda saw it,

right there in the back yard.

"A monster!" she said.

"An awful, scary monster!"

"Where?" said Oliver.

"There," said Amanda.

"Why, Amanda," said Father.

"That is only a bush."

"And anyway," said Oliver,

"there are no such things as monsters."

"Of course not," said Mother.

"Come, my big girl. I will tuck you in."

I am a big girl, thought Amanda.

There are no such things as monsters.

I won't think about it.

But as soon as the lights were out,

Amanda knew.

There was a monster in her room.

It was hiding in the closet.

Or the toy box.

Or maybe under her bed.

Yes, that was it.

If she tried to get up,

it would grab her by the foot.

Amanda squeezed Sallie Rabbit tight.

She lay very still.

She didn't even breathe.

Maybe the monster

wouldn't notice her.

But her heart was going

ka-boom, ka-boom.

The monster would hear it.

KA-BOOM, KA-BOOM.

KA-BOOOM! KA-BOOOM!

"Mother!" cried Amanda.

"Father! Come here!"

Mother and Father came running.

"What is it?" asked Mother.

"An awful, scary monster,"

said Amanda.

"I think it's under my bed."

Father shone his flashlight

under her bed.

"No one there," he said.

"Besides, there are no such things

as monsters. Remember?"

"Well, it was there,"

whispered Amanda.

Mother held Amanda tight.

"It's all right, my sweet potato,"

she said. "I am here."

And she sat in the rocking chair

next to Amanda's bed

until she fell asleep.

THE ROCKING CHAIR

"Boo!" cried Oliver the next day.

Everywhere Amanda went,

he jumped out at her.

"I'm an awful, scary monster,"

he cackled. "Hee, hee, hee!"

At lunchtime, under the table,

he grabbed her foot.

"Stop that," said Amanda.

"It's just a little monster," said Oliver.

When his friend James came over,

they played Monster Tag.

"We're going to get you!"

cried Oliver and James.

Amanda ran away.

But at bedtime,

Oliver came to her room.

"Leave me alone!" said Amanda.

"I'm doing a monster check,"

said Oliver.

He looked in the closet

and inside the toy box

and under her bed.

"Not a single monster," said Oliver.

"And do you know why?"

"Why?" asked Amanda.

"Because there are no monsters,"

said Oliver.

"Not in the whole entire world."

Father looked under the bed again,

just to make sure.

Mother gave Amanda extra hugs.

"Good night, my brave girl," she said.

I am brave, thought Amanda.

There are no monsters.

Not in the whole entire world.

And besides,

Father looked under the bed.

But as soon as Mother and Father

were gone, Amanda knew.

There was a monster in her room.

She opened one eye.

And there it was,

sitting in the rocking chair.

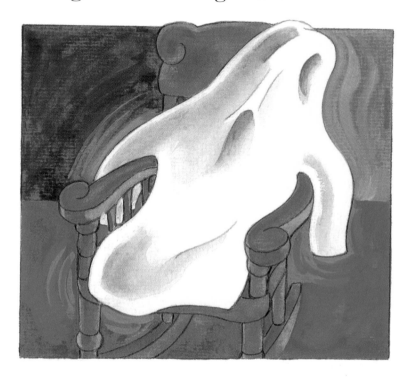

Amanda dove down under the covers.

KA-BOOM! KA-BOOM!

What should she do?

If she called Mother and Father,

the monster would get her for sure.

She listened.

The monster didn't make a sound.

She peeked out.

The monster didn't move.

Maybe it was asleep.

"One, two, three," counted Amanda.

"Go!"

She jumped out of bed.

She ran as fast as she could,

out the door,

down the hall,

to Mother and Father's room.

But at their door, Amanda stopped.

Should she wake them up?

If she did, they would know

she wasn't a brave girl after all.

Suddenly Amanda felt very tired.

She lay down in front of their door.

In a minute she was asleep.

"What's this?" said Father

in the morning.

"The awful, scary monster came back,"

said Amanda.

Father carried Amanda to her room.

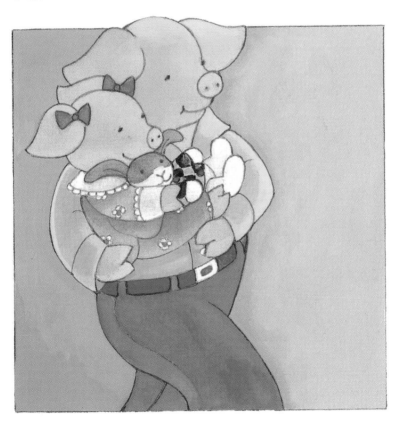

"Is that a monster sitting

in your rocking chair?" he asked.

"Oh!" said Amanda. "No.

It's only my bathrobe."

THE TRAP

"What you need," said Oliver,

"is a monster trap.

Even though there are no monsters,

in case one comes to your room,

you can capture it."

"Will you help me build one?"

asked Amanda.

"Of course," said Oliver.

He went to his room

and got a lot of his toys and his tools

and his big box of blocks.

"Now," he said, "we are ready to build."

"The monster might come in the door,"

said Amanda. "Or the window."

"First we will take care of the window,"

said Oliver.

He piled his trucks

and Amanda's tea cups

and a jar full of marbles

on the window sill.

"If a monster tries to get in," he said,

"there will be a big crash.

That monster will be so scared,

he will run away."

"That's good," said Amanda.

"Now for the trap," said Oliver.

He dumped all his blocks

out of the box.

"We'll start by building a block tower,"

he said, "next to the door."

Oliver and Amanda began to build.

Soon the tower was as tall as Amanda.

"How big is this monster anyway?"

asked Oliver.

"Bigger than me," said Amanda.

They built some more.

Soon the tower was as tall as Oliver.

"Bigger than you," said Amanda.

They kept building.

They used up all the blocks.

Oliver stood on his tiptoes.

He put books on top,

and games and his parking garage

and his lawn mower.

"Is that big enough?" he asked.

"I think so," said Amanda.

Oliver stood on Amanda's stool.

He put the block box

upside down on top of the tower.

"Now," he said,

"the monster trap is ready."

"How does it work?" asked Amanda.

"Simple," said Oliver.

"If a monster opens the door,

the block tower tips over

and the box falls down

and the monster is stuck in the box."

Amanda smiled.

"I like my monster trap," she said.

"Let's show Mother and Father."

"You can't do that," said Oliver.

"Why not?" asked Amanda.

"Stop!" cried Oliver.

"Don't open the door!"

But Amanda had already opened
the door.

"Oops!" she said.

The door hit the block tower.

The tower tipped over.

The box fell down.

Right on top of Oliver.

"Help!" he cried. "I'm stuck!"

Amanda dug him out.

"My trap worked," she said.

"I caught a monster."

A MONSTER POEM

"It's amazing," said Mother,

"how many things you can do.

You can make cookies and set the table

and even reach the sink.

Without standing on a stool."

"And I can count to a hundred,"
said Amanda, "and almost read
and ride my new bike.
Without training wheels."
"My oh my," said Mother.
"You are almost grown up."

At bedtime,

Oliver came to Amanda's room again.

"Monster Patrol!" he said.

He looked in the dress-up box

and behind the bookcase

and inside her Bake Easy play oven.

"Now, repeat after me," he said.

"There are no monsters.

Never have been, never will be. Really."

"There are no monsters," said Amanda.

"Never have been, never will be. Really."

Father gave Amanda a flashlight

to put under her pillow.

Mother whispered in her ear,

"Remember, you are almost grown up."

I am almost grown up, thought Amanda.

There are no monsters.

Never have been, never will be. Really.

She smiled.

Now she could go to sleep.

But as soon as Amanda closed her eyes,

she knew.

There was a monster in her room.

It was hiding behind the curtains.

Or under the rocking chair.

Or somewhere.

She could feel it out there in the dark.

Amanda squeezed Sallie Rabbit

so tight, she nearly popped her stuffing.

KA-BOOM! KA-BOOM! KA-BOOM!

I can reach the sink, she thought.

I can ride my bike

without training wheels.

I am big.

Suddenly Amanda felt

a poem coming on.

She sat straight up in bed.

She said very loud,

"I am too big a pig

to be scared of a little monster.

So boo to you!

Go away! Shoo!

Anyway, there is no such thing as you."

She shone Father's flashlight
all around.

At the closet and the curtains

and the rocking chair

and everywhere.

"Not a single monster," she said.

Then she turned off the flashlight

and went to sleep.

"Guess what," said Amanda

in the morning.

"There are no monsters.

Never have been, never will be. Really."

Mother and Father smiled.

"I knew that," said Oliver.